For Ste xx

OXFORD
UNIVERSITY PRESS

Great Clarendon Street, Oxford OX2 6DP

Oxford University Press is a department of the University of Oxford.
It furthers the University's objective of excellence in research, scholarship,
and education by publishing worldwide in

Oxford New York

Athens Auckland Bangkok Bogotá Buenos Aires Calcutta
Cape Town Chennai Dar es Salaam Delhi Florence Hong Kong Istanbul
Karachi Kuala Lumpur Madrid Melbourne Mexico City Mumbai
Nairobi Paris São Paulo Shanghai Singapore Taipei Tokyo Toronto Warsaw
with associated companies in Berlin Ibadan

Oxford is a registered trade mark of Oxford University Press
in the UK and in certain other countries

Copyright © Joanne Partis 2001

The moral rights of the artist have been asserted

Database right Oxford University Press (maker)

First published 2001

1 3 5 7 9 10 8 6 4 2

British Library Cataloguing in Publication Data available

ISBN 0–19–279060–9 (hardback)
ISBN 0–19–272454–1 (paperback)

Printed in Malaysia

Stripe's
Naughty Sister

Joanne Partis

OXFORD
UNIVERSITY PRESS

Stripe wanted to play with his
friends but instead he had to look
after his little sister.

'Play with me,' she said.
'No,' said Stripe. If he couldn't play
with his friends, he was going to
doze in the sun. But the moment his
back was turned . . .

. . . his little sister disappeared. Stripe would be in so much trouble! He had to find her. He set off to catch her before she went too far away.

Oh no! Stripe's sister ran into a patch of prickly cactuses. As she was small, she easily wove her way through.

But Stripe was bigger and it was hard squeezing between the spiky plants.

OUCH!

He heard giggling and looked up just in
time to see his sister running off.

Stripe caught up, to see his
little sister grab some
creeper and swing across
a muddy swamp.

Stripe was cross, but he
had to follow her.

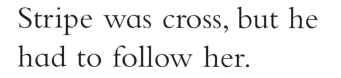

The creeper creaked and . . .

GLOOP!

The creeper broke and Stripe
splashed into the swamp.

Stripe's sister was having a lovely time. She found a hollow tree and dived inside to explore.

Stripe caught up with her. But he was too big for the hole. THUD! Stripe bumped his head.

Stripe's sister had climbed
high up the tree. She looked
down at Stripe.
But he had had enough.

'I'm prickly and I'm muddy
and I'm sore,' he said. 'And
I'm going home.'

Behind him, Stripe could hear squeaking.
He tried to take no notice. At last, he looked
around. His sister was still at the top of the tree.

'I'm stuck,' she cried.

Stripe knew he couldn't leave her. He knew
what a big brother must do.

Carefully he climbed up the tree,

higher and higher, until he reached his little sister.

But now they were both stuck. Stripe didn't
know how to get down. Below him, he heard
a **cracking** noise and . . .

. . . down

down

down down they fell.

OOMPH!

His little sister landed on top of him – hard!

'Thank you for helping me get down,'
she said. 'You're the best brother in the world,'
and she licked his nose.

Stripe felt happy. They set off for home and, that night, tired after their adventures, they went straight to sleep.